Dear Parent:

Congratulations! Your child is taking the first steps on an exciting journey. The destination? Independent reading!

STEP INTO READING® will help your child get there. The program offers five steps to reading success. Each step includes fun stories and colorful art. There are also Step into Reading Sticker Books, Step into Reading Math Readers, Step into Reading Write-In Readers, Step into Reading Phonics Readers, and Step into Reading Phonics First Steps! Boxed Sets—a complete literacy program with something for every child.

Learning to Read, Step by Step!

Ready to Read Preschool–Kindergarten
• big type and easy words • rhyme and rhythm • picture clues
For children who know the alphabet and are eager to begin reading.

Reading with Help Preschool–Grade 1
• basic vocabulary • short sentences • simple stories
For children who recognize familiar words and sound out new words with help.

Reading on Your Own Grades 1–3
• engaging characters • easy-to-follow plots • popular topics
For children who are ready to read on their own.

Reading Paragraphs Grades 2–3
• challenging vocabulary • short paragraphs • exciting stories
For newly independent readers who read simple sentences with confidence.

Ready for Chapters Grades 2–4
• chapters • longer paragraphs • full-color art
For children who want to take the plunge into chapter books but still like colorful pictures.

STEP INTO READING® is designed to give every child a successful reading experience. The grade levels are only guides. Children can progress through the steps at their own speed, developing confidence in their reading, no matter what their grade.

Remember, a lifetime love of reading starts with a single step!

For Frankie and Kevin
—M.L.

 Published in the United States by Random House Children's Books, a division of Random House, Inc., New York, and in Canada by Random House of Canada Limited, Toronto, in conjunction with Disney Enterprises, Inc.

Visit us on the Web!

www.stepintoreading.com

www.randomhouse.com/kids/disney

Educators and librarians, for a variety of teaching tools, visit us at

www.randomhouse.com/teachers

Library of Congress Cataloging-in-Publication Data
Lagonegro, Melissa.
Roadwork! — 1st ed.
p. cm.— (Step into reading)
ISBN 978-0-7364-2516-2 (trade)
ISBN 978-0-7364-8059-8 (lib. bdg.)
I. Cars (Motion picture) II. Title. III. Title: Roadwork!
PZ7.L14317Ro 2008
2007024584

Printed in the United States of America 10 9 8 7 6 5 4 3 2 1 First Edition

STEP INTO READING®

ROADWORK!

By Melissa Lagonegro
Illustrated by Art Mawhinney

Random House New York

New cars are coming
to Radiator Springs.
They want to see
Lightning McQueen!

The town is
getting ready.
They have work to do!

McQueen paves the road.
It will be smooth
for his fans.

Ramone gives himself a fresh coat of paint.

He is ready to paint
all the new cars
that come to town.

Sarge leads
his own boot camp.

He will get
all the 4x4s that visit
into good shape.

Fillmore makes
his own fuel.
He hopes
McQueen's fans
are thirsty.

TASTE-IN

Rust-eze
95
Rust-eze
95
95

At Casa Della Tires,
Luigi has
new tires to sell.
McQueen tries them on.

Guido helps, too.
He is a busy forklift.

Flo runs the diner.
Cars visit and sip oil
with friends.

Soon it will be packed
with racing fans.

Red waters the flowers.
He wants the town
to look its best!

Sally fixes up her motel.
It is the perfect place
for guests to rest.

Frank cuts
and harvests grain.
Mater gets Frank to
work extra hard.

Sheriff puts up
new road signs.

He does not want
anyone to speed.

After a long drive,
the cars need a tune-up.
Doc is ready to take
good care of them.

Lizzie gets
new bumper stickers.
She will sell them
in her shop.

Kori reports
the latest news.
Rust-eze

Al Oft,

the Lightyear blimp,

flies overhead.

He lets everyone
in town know
when visitors are
on their way.

Flo's
V8
Cafe
Rust-eze
95

The town is ready
and the work is done!
The cars go out
and have some fun!

Welcome to
Radiator Springs!